To Helen and Ruth,
the best friends anyone could ever have,
J.C.

TUSK TROUBLE

by Jane Clarke and Cecilia Johansson

British Library Cataloguing in Publication Data

A catalogue record of this book is available from the British Library.

ISBN 0 340 87725 1 (HB)

ISBN 0340 86079 0 (PB)

Text copyright © Jane Clarke 2003

Illustrations copyright © Cecilia Johansson 2003

The right of Jane Clarke to be identified as the author and Cecilia Johansson
as the illustrator of this Work has been asserted by them in accordance with
the Copyright, Designs and Patents Act 1988.

first edition published 2003

10 9 8 7 6 5 4 3 2

Published by Hodder Children's Books
a division of Hodder Headline Limited
338 Euston Road London NW1 3BH

Printed in Hong Kong

Awarded for excellence
to Arts & Libraries

Kent
County
Council

Tusk Trouble

Written by Jane Clarke

Illustrated by Cecilia Johansson

Hodder
Children's
Books

A division of Hodder Headline Limited

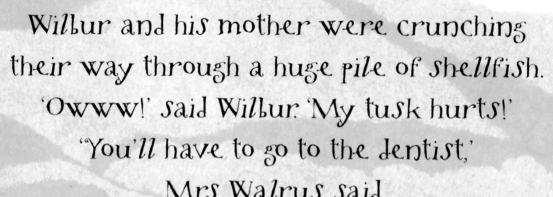

Wilbur and his mother were crunching
their way through a huge pile of shellfish.
'Owww!' said Wilbur. 'My tusk hurts!'
"You'll have to go to the dentist,'
Mrs Walrus said.

'I don't want to go
to the dentist,'
said Wilbur.

'My tusk only hurts when I crunch,'
said Wilbur. 'If I take the shells
off, I can suck them.'

'Have some seaweed,' said Mrs Walrus.
'It's *lovely* and soft.'
'Ugh!' said Wilbur. 'I don't want to eat
seaweed. It's green and *slimy*.'
'Then *you'll* have to go to the
dentist,' said Mrs Walrus.
'I don't want to go to the
dentist,' said Wilbur.

Wilbur's friends were tusk wrestling.
Wilbur loved tusk wrestling.
He locked tusks with
his friend Walter.

Whump!

'OWWW!' yelled Wilbur. 'My tusk hurts!'
'You'll have to go to the dentist,'
Walter said.
'I don't want to go to the
dentist,' said Wilbur.

'My tusk only hurts when I wrestle,' said Wilbur.
'Let's play on the ice slide with Wanda.'

Wheee!

Wanda, Wilbur and Walter
swooped down the slide.

splash!

They somersaulted into the sea.

'That was great!
Let's do it again!' Walter said.

Walter stabbed his tusks into the ice
and pulled himself up on to the ice floe.

Wanda stabbed her tusks into the ice
and pulled herself up on to the ice floe.
Wilbur stabbed his tusks into the ice and...
'Owww!' yelled Wilbur.
'My tusk hurts!'
'You'll have to go to the dentist,'
Wanda said.

'I don't want to go to
the dentist,' said Wilbur.

'I'll swim to Grandpa's,' Wilbur said.
'It's easy to get out there. He's got
a landing slope.'
It was a long way to Grandpa's.
Wilbur's tusk hurt in the cold water.
He hauled himself up Grandpa's landing
slope and lay there whimpering.

'Tsk, tsk,' said Grandpa. He put his flipper around Wilbur's shoulders and helped him up on to the ice floe. 'Whatever is the matter?'

'My tusk hurts,' wailed Wilbur. His whiskers quivered.

'You'll have to go to the dentist,' Grandpa said.

'I don't want to go to the dentist,'
said Wilbur.

Grandpa smiled. 'Nor did I,' he said.

Mrs Walrus lumbered
up the landing slope
towards them.
'Walter and Wanda
said I'd find you
here,' she said.
'Is your tusk
still hurting?'

'Yes,' said Wilbur. 'I'll have
to go to the dentist!'
'At *last!*' said
Mrs Walrus.

Miss Tusker the dentist was very gentle.

'I see what the problem is,' she said. 'You've got a piece of shell stuck in the top of your tusk. There! I've taken it out.' 'That feels much better!' said Wilbur.

'If you brush your tusks twice a day with this special fish-flavoured toothpaste, your tusks will be strong and shiny,' said Miss Tusker.

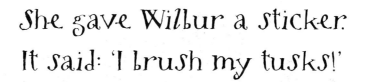

She gave Wilbur a sticker.
It said: 'I brush my tusks!'

'Wow!' said Grandpa. 'I wish I had
tusks like yours.'
'Miss Tusker will make you a false
tusk,' said Wilbur. 'You'll have
to go to the dentist.'
'I don't want to go to the dentist!'
said Grandpa.
'Tsk, tsk,' said Wilbur. He put his
flipper around Grandpa's shoulder.
'If I can go to the dentist,
so can you!'